A MAGIC MICRO™ ADVENTURE

The Cats of Castle Mountain

A MAGIC MICRO™ ADVENTURE

The Cats of Castle Mountain

by

Eileen Buckholtz

and

Ruth Glick

Illustrations by Bert Dodson
Cover by Bradley Clark

A Parachute Press Book

Scholastic Inc.

New York Toronto London Auckland Sydney

For our cats: Brandy, Carrie, Friday, and Lion

ISBN 0-590-33479-4

Copyright © 1985 by Parachute Press
All rights reserved. Published by Scholastic Inc.

12 11 10 9 8 7 6 5 4 3 2 1   1   6 7 8 9/8 0 1/9

Printed in the U.S.A.   28

The programs in this book will run on these computers:

*IBM PC

*IBM PCjr.

*APPLE II+

*APPLE IIe

*COMMODORE 64

*VIC 20

*ATARI 400/800

*RADIO SHACK COLOR COMPUTER

*RADIO SHACK TRS-80

You are the star of the story!
You have the Magic Micro . . .

Your computer is about to take you into a world of adventure and excitement. The power of the Magic Micro is at your fingertips. All you need is your computer, the programs in this book, and a sense of adventure!

There are just a few rules. The programs in the book are in BASIC. So make sure you know how to put your computer in BASIC before you begin.

You must add a few lines to each program to make it run on your computer. When you come to a program in the story, type it just the way it appears. Then turn to the Magic Scroll section on page 64. You will have to add three or four more lines that are just for *your* computer. The Magic Scroll will tell you which lines to add — and sometimes there will be lines you have to take out.

Remember, you must type the programs exactly right. Even an extra space can make a difference. If you have trouble, put the program on your screen by using the LIST command. Check that version against the program in the book. Also, remember to type NEW before you start a new program. That clears out any leftovers from old programs. That's all there is to it.

Now your adventure can begin.

Chapter 1

Beep, beep, beep.

Your eyes pop open. Why is your alarm ringing? This is Saturday. And it's so early in the morning that the sun isn't even up.

Your gray and white tomcat, sleeping at the foot of the bed, wakes up and meows. He thinks it's breakfast time. But all you want to do is snuggle back under the covers.

However, the beeping is getting louder. You suddenly realize it's not coming from your alarm clock. It's your Magic Micro on the dresser.

When you hit the screen display button, it asks: *Want to go on an adventure?*

"Call me in a couple of hours," you yawn.

But the Red Queen is in the first house and Leo is rising. If we don't go now, we'll miss the excitement, it says.

Even though it doesn't make any sense, it sounds interesting. But the cat doesn't agree. He jumps up on your chest and paws at your nose to get your attention.

"Just let me feed the cat first," you protest.

I'll wait, the Magic Micro agrees.

Three minutes later your cat is contentedly chomping a bowl of Ranch House Mackerel and you're dressed and ready.

Here we go! says your Magic Micro.

If you're ready for another amazing adventure with your Magic Micro, then type the following program into your computer. When you have typed in these lines, turn to pages 64-67 and type in the lines listed for your computer. Then run the program. Answer the computer when it asks, "Where are you going?" by typing in the answer, "Castle Mountain."

Continued on the next page.

PROGRAM 1

```
10 REM MAGIC TRANSPORT PROGRAM
20 PRINT "WHERE ARE WE GOING?"
30 INPUT P$
40 GOSUB 960:GOSUB 900
50 FOR I=1 TO 150
60 RX=MU:GOSUB 930
70 GOSUB 980
80 RX=SH:GOSUB 930:VT=RD
90 RX=SW:GOSUB 930:HT=RD
100 GOSUB 910
110 RX=AC:GOSUB 930
120 PRINT CHR$(RD+AS)
130 NEXT I
140 VT=1:HT=1:GOSUB 910
150 PRINT "YOU ARE NOW IN ";P$
160 END
```

You are pulled into a world of eerie sounds and flashing lights, as your Magic Micro whisks you away to a strange new land.

When the screen clears, you're standing in a grassy meadow. You pick up the Magic Micro beside you and put it inside your jacket. Behind you is a pine forest that stretches into the distance. At the other edge of the meadow is a rugged mountain with rocks and ledges and caves. And off to your right is a beautiful castle. Colorful flags flutter from the turrets, and the silvery roof glitters in the late-afternoon sun.

It's almost like a scene from a storybook. The carpet of grass under your feet is studded with tiny, colorful flowers. The forest behind you is shadowy and forbidding.

Suddenly you get a spooky feeling. You feel as if you're being watched.

You glance at the forest. Not even a pine needle is stirring. Turning toward the mountain, you study the rocky terrain. You'd swear that *something* was flitting behind the boulders and in the openings of the caves. And you're almost sure you caught the glint of yellow eyes from the darkness of a rocky overhang. But when it comes right down to it, there's really nothing to see. It must just be your imagination. Or maybe it's the shadow of a cloud. You glance up and notice that the sky is clear blue — not a cloud anywhere. So much for that theory. Maybe you'd better just be on your way.

You've taken a few steps in the direction of the castle when you hear a small sound. It's almost like the meowing of your cat at home when he wants your attention.

You turn around. Running across the meadow toward you is a little orange tiger kitten. His tail is standing up straight in the air and waving like a high-flying flag. You know cats well enough to understand that's a sure sign he wants to be friends.

"Hey, fella, where did you come from?" you ask.

"Meow!"

You didn't expect a real answer.

The kitten bats at the leg of your jeans and then starts patting hopefully at the laces of your tennis shoes.

"Want to play? Is that it? Sorry, but I didn't bring any cat toys along."

That doesn't faze the kitten. He prances off into the forest, then comes back with a pine twig and drops it at your feet.

"Okay," you laugh. You pick up the twig and swish it around on the ground just the way you would for your own cat. The little kitten pounces on the needles and tears into them with his claws. Then he backs off to get a running start to do it again.

"You're a real tiger," you praise him.

"Meow!"

You dangle the twig in the air, and he jumps for it. When you raise it higher, he does a leap that would make an Olympic athlete proud.

This is fun. You're so caught up in the game that you jump in surprise when you hear an angry hiss beind you. You whirl around and find yourself facing a full-grown white and orange cat. Her back is arched. Her tail is puffed out and lashing back and forth, and her eyes are flashing. You bet she's this kitten's mother. And she doesn't seem pleased about her kitten's new playmate. In fact, she looks as if she'd like to tear you to pieces.

Chapter 2

You start to back away. "Listen, I wasn't going to hurt your kitten. Honest," you try to explain.

"Why should I believe you?" she hisses between clenched teeth. "You're probably a spy for the Red Queen."

"I don't even know who the Red Queen is," you say. Then your mouth drops open. Are you really having a conversation with a cat?

"Wow! You can talk!" you gasp.

"Stop trying to change the subject," the mom cat snaps back. "I want answers now."

Out of the corner of your eye, you notice dozens of cats with their heads poked out from behind rocks. Gray cats, black cats, white cats — every variation of cat fur you've ever imagined. And by the look of confidence in the mother cat's eyes, you realize she knows the odds are in her favor.

"Mom, please, we were only playing," the kitten protests. "Everyone knows that the Red Queen doesn't play around."

"Hush, Leo," the mother scolds. "You don't know what kind of nasty plot the Red Queen Cerise might be hatching."

Just then, a loud siren blast splits the air. At the same time, at the top of the mountain, a revolving warning light starts to flash. It reminds you of the lights you've seen on top of police cars.

"The Red Queen is coming," a black cat shouts.

The cats disappear so fast that you wonder for a moment if they were ever

really there. The mom cat springs into action. She grabs Leo by the scruff of the neck and dashes back for the rocks at the base of the mountain.

Quicker than you can blink an eye, you're alone. You can see an elaborate gold coach crossing the castle's drawbridge. It's pulled by snarling Doberman pinschers.

The coach is drawing dangerously near. You want to run. But you don't know where to go. And your legs are shaking so much that you don't know if they'll move.

Suddenly, you feel a frantic tug on the leg of your jeans. It's Leo.

"Come on," he urges. "Run."

His words somehow unlock your frozen muscles. The two of you dash back toward the rocks. Before you know it, Leo has led you to a crack in the mountainside that forms an almost invisible entrance right into the mountain. Inside are dozens of cats. Some are shivering and hanging back from the mouth of the cave. A few bolder ones are peering out into the meadow.

From your hiding place, you also sneak a look at the clearing. The golden coach has pulled to a stop. The door swings open, and out steps a tall, pale woman. Her long, dark hair hangs down around her shoulders. Her face is so white she looks as if she uses chalk dust for makeup. And she's definitely overdressed for a visit to the countryside. She's wearing a blood-red velvet gown trimmed with black fur.

The queen turns her dark gaze toward the mountain. It seems for a moment as if her piercing eyes are looking directly at you. You can't help shivering and taking a step back into the shadows.

"I know you're in there. Come out, you miserable cats, or I'm coming in to get you," she snarls. Behind her, the Dobermans are growling.

"Never," a large gray cat in back of you mutters. "We'll never surrender. We don't want to be your slaves like all the other animals in the kingdom."

The queen waits for a moment. When there's no response, she stalks across the meadow toward the cave. Suddenly, a shield drops down in front of the mouth of the cave. It shimmers with a rainbow of delicate colors. When Queen Cerise tries to pass through it, she is bounced backward and lands sprawled out on her back.

When she gets up, her eyes are blazing. You hear her mutter under her breath.

"What happened?" you ask.

"It's our force field," Leo explains. "It comes down to protect us when she gets near the mountain. It is powered by energy from the stars. But I don't know if it will hold this time, because the last few nights have been so cloudy."

The queen also seems to be wondering about the strength of the force field. You watch as she cautiously reapproaches the shimmering curtain. This time, instead of trying to plow through, she takes off her red shoe and pokes its three-inch spike heel at the shimmering barrier. To your horror, the point of the heel goes right through.

"Aha!" she cackles, and then she continues to jab at the barrier with her spike heel.

"Oh, no! What are we going to do?" several cats wail. "If she gets through, we're done for."

As if to add to the feeling of impending doom, the sun has gone down and the clearing has been plunged into dark shadows. The wind starts to howl and a cold shiver runs up and down your spine.

"If only the stars would come out. Then we'd be saved," Leo's mother says.

Well, this was certainly a quick adventure, you think. And it looks as if it might be your last. Just then, you hear your Magic Micro beep inside your jacket. You pull it out and eagerly push the button. The words "Get me out of here" are trembling on your lips.

But before you can voice them, the Magic Micro says:

There's a chance we can strengthen the force field and keep the queen out for now.

"But that's impossible!" you say.

It won't be easy, but it's not impossible, beeps the Magic Micro.

Chapter 3

"What will stop the queen?" you ask eagerly.

If we can make the stars come out, their light will give the force field energy.

Carefully type the following program into your computer. (Lines 90, 100, and 200 must each be typed as one line.) When you have typed these lines, turn to pages 68-70 and type in the lines listed for your computer. When you have finished typing, run the program. You'll need to do some adding to make the force field strong enough to keep Queen Cerise out. Turn to the Magic Scroll on page 70 for instructions.

PROGRAM 2

```
10  GOSUB 960
20  GOSUB 900
30  VT=1:HT=1:GOSUB 910
40  RX=20:GOSUB 930:D1=RD
50  RX=10:GOSUB 930:D2=RD
60  PRINT D1;" + ";D2;" = "
70  INPUT K
80  IF K=D1+D2 THEN 120
90  PRINT "SORRY, RIGHT ANSWER
    IS ";D1+D2
100 PRINT "NO MORE STARS FOR YOU
    TONIGHT"
110 END
120 VT=2:GOSUB 910:PRINT "     "
130 FOR I=1 TO K
140 RX=SW-1:GOSUB 930:HT=RD
150 RX=SH-3:GOSUB 930:VT=RD+2
160 GOSUB 910:PRINT "*"
170 NEXT I
180 T1=T1+K
190 IF T1<100 THEN 30
200 PRINT "FORCE FIELD 100%
    POWER"
210 END
```

The whole time you've been working frantically, the queen has been poking furiously with that wicked-looking spike heel. But now it's obvious that she can feel the force field strengthen. And it's making her angry!

"I know a little magic," she mutters. "Maybe a magic spell will do the trick." She takes a step back and raises her hands. In a frightening voice, she begins to chant, "With the power of wind . . . with the strength of a wave . . . I will force my way into your nasty cat cave!"

You see lightning flash from the tips of her red fingernails. It looks as if she's going to get through after all.

"Poke, stroke, go up in smoke," she adds for good measure.

A bolt of lightning shoots from her finger and hits the force field. You gasp. But instead of shattering the field, it arches like a boomerang back in the queen's direction. She sees it coming and jumps aside, but not in time. The fire hits the fur at the edge of her gown. She squeaks in alarm. Something about her reminds you of a mouse with its tail caught in a trap.

The cats meow enthusiastically. Some

of them even come out from behind the rocks and parade back and forth with their tails in the air, now that they know she can't touch them.

Queen Cerise isn't amused. In fact, she's boiling mad. "All right, my unruly cats, you may have bought yourself a little time," she concedes. "But it won't make a bit of difference in the grand scheme of things. Your days of freedom are numbered. You'll find I still have plenty of tricks up my sleeve."

Then she whirls around and marches back to her coach. A moment later, she cracks a whip and the dogs obey her cruel command. The coach lurches forward as they head back toward the castle.

There's a collective sigh of relief from the cats. "Well done," says a deep voice behind you. You turn to find yourself facing a gray and white tiger cat. He's one of the largest cats you've ever seen. You'd be afraid, except that the kind look in his eyes tells you he means no harm. The fur around his muzzle is white, and you have the feeling he's very old.

"That's Augustus, our leader," Leo whispers.

"You have saved the Cats of Castle Mountain from the Red Queen," Augustus says to you. "You have proved yourself a friend."

"Yes," the rest of the group agree. One by one, they come up to thank you, and each cat tells you his or her name. There are dozens of them, but several stand out.

Caesar is a round, white cat with a habit of washing his front paw after he speaks. Isis is a small, golden female whose whiskers twitch as she inspects you. Brutus and Justinian could be twins. They're both lean and gray, but Justinian's eyes are green and Brutus's are orange. Both look tough, like veterans of many skirmishes. You're glad you're on the same side that they are.

One of the last cats to introduce herself is Victoria, Leo's mother.

"I'm so sorry I misjudged you," she

apologizes. "Please come into our humble home. You are most welcome here."

You're about to follow her down the tunnel when you notice a sleek black cat with deep green eyes sitting by herself. None of the others are paying any attention to her. She looks sad. And yet there's something very regal about her, too. You want to know who she is and why she's by herself.

"I've met everyone else. But who are you?" you ask.

She smiles sadly and sits up straighter. "I am Cassandra. The others stay away from me because I have a powerful gift."

"But that should make them like you."

She shakes her head. "My gift is that I can see into the future. And often the other cats do not want to know what is in store for them. But it is my duty to tell them."

You understand why she is so alone. Knowing the future must be a terrible burden.

The others go down the tunnel into the heart of Castle Mountain. You turn away from Cassandra and follow. The tunnel is really a strange place. It's not like any cave you've heard of before. For one thing, it's not dark. There's a soft glowing light that seems to shine right out of the rock. And it's not cold or damp. You can feel warm air gently wafting through the passage-ways as if there's some sort of heating system deep inside the mountain.

As you walk, you feel Leo rubbing against your leg every so often. It's obvious that he considers you his personal discovery. And you've become pretty fond of the little guy, too. Yet there's one thing you're still curious about.

"Leo, if you and the other cats can talk, why were you just playing charades with me out in the meadow?" you ask, ducking down to avoid hitting your head on a beam.

"Because I'm not supposed to talk to strangers," he answers.

Just then you round a corner and find yourself in a large cavern.

"This is our living room," Victoria explains. You look around, hiding a grin. This place was obviously furnished with cats in mind. In fact, it looks like cat heaven. The floor is covered with thick, yellow carpet that is badly scratched in lots of places. On it is an assortment of cardboard boxes and laundry baskets — just the things cats like to curl up in. And there are carpeted poles and multilevel shelves all over the large room. It's just like a cat jungle gym you might see in a pet store window — only bigger and better. It's perfect for the kind of climbing and jumping and relaxing that cats do. As you watch, the cats scatter around the room, climbing the poles and arranging themselves on the shelves, or settling down comfortably in the baskets. Everybody seems to have a favorite spot.

"Where did all this come from?" you ask.

"It's always been here," Augustus explains. "But the legends tell us that the Masters who once inhabited this land left it here for us. They had to go away, but they made sure we were taken care of."

"They even left us a defense system," Caesar adds, pausing to lick his paw after he speaks.

"And that's kept us safe from the Red Queen," Leo pipes up from his perch near your head.

There's a general meowing of agreement from everyone — except Cassandra. You see her standing in the doorway. She doesn't say anything, but the look in her green eyes tells you that if she did, her words would not be reassuring. As you watch, she turns and pads silently away.

But you forget all about Cassandra when the cats start playing in the living room. It's fun to watch them dash up and down the poles, jump from platform to platform, and pounce on the rubber mice scattered about on the carpet.

"This place is really neat," you tell Leo. "What else is inside the mountain?"

"If you like this, you'll love our sun room," he says. As he speaks, he leads you through an archway into another large area. It is full of tropical plants growing out of natural rock formations. In the center of the room is a little stream with stepping stones. And you'd swear that the sun was shining brightly — except that the warm light is coming from the rocky ceiling. Several cats are stretched out, basking in the warm glow from above.

It all looks so relaxing that you almost want to lie down yourself. Or maybe you'll get a drink from the clear, sparkling stream the way a large calico cat is doing.

You take a step in that direction, when the cat at the stream gasps. "Yuck!" he shouts. "This water tastes terrible — like rotten eggs!"

"What's the matter?" someone asks. Suddenly the sleepy cats spring up, alert and on their guard. They gather around.

"What's wrong?" Augustus hurries into the room. He tastes the water. "There is a strange taste of sulphur in this water," he says. "This is not our pure drinking water."

Nobody seems to know what has happened. At that moment, you look up to see Cassandra perched on a rock on the other side of the stream. She meows, and everyone looks in her direction. A hush falls over the room as the cats wait for her to speak.

"This is the work of the Red Queen," she announces.

"But how could that be?" Caesar asks. "She isn't even here."

"She doesn't have to be," Cassandra explains. "I had a vision. I know what happened."

Dramatically, she waits for a few moments before she starts to speak again. "Queen Cerise has found the spring that supplies our water," she says. "She has

made our water undrinkable. Without water, we will be weak and unable to fight off her coming invasion."

"Oh, this is terrible!" the golden cat, Isis, wails. "We must have water, or we will die."

"What are we going to do?" several cats ask at once. There is so much confusion in the room that you don't see Leo wander away.

"Can your special vision help us, Cassandra?" Augustus asks.

For the first time, the sleek black cat looks uncertain. "I think the solution lies with the filtering system the Masters left us," she murmurs. "If we could only adjust it, we could neutralize the chemical Queen Cerise has put into our water. But I fear it is too difficult."

"Maybe I can help," you volunteer.

All eyes turn in your direction. Suddenly you feel uncertain. The Magic Micro senses your doubt.

Don't worry. We can do it, it says.

Type the following program into your computer. (Lines 10, 20, 60, 130, and 150 must each be typed as one line.) When you have typed in these lines, turn to pages 71-73 and type in the lines listed for your computer. Then run the program. You have seven chances to adjust the water filter. The Magic Scroll on page 73 will tell you how to do it.

PROGRAM 3

```
10 M1$="TOO HIGH--NOW TOO MUCH
   BASE IN THE WATER"
20 M2$="TOO LOW--DANGEROUS ACID
   STILL IN WATER"
30 NG=6
40 GOSUB 900:GOSUB 960:
50 RX=100:GOSUB 930:X=RD
60 PRINT "SET THE DIAL ON A
   NUMBER BETWEEN 1 AND 100"
70 INPUT S
80 IF S=X THEN 130
90 G=G+1:IF G>NG THEN 150
100 IF S>X THEN PRINT M1$
110 IF S < X THEN PRINT M2$
120 GOTO 60
130 PRINT "SUCCESS! THE FILTERING
    SYSTEM IS NOW WORKING"
140 END
150 PRINT "THE DIAL HAS BROKEN
    OFF IN YOUR HAND":END
```

"Hey, you did it!" Justinian exclaims. But most of the other cats are more cautious. Maybe it worked and maybe it didn't. But nobody wants to be the first to try it.

Finally you look up to see Cassandra walking deliberately toward the water. Casually she bends down to the stream, sticks out her delicate pink tongue, and begins to lap at the water. There isn't a sound in the room besides the gurgling of the stream and the *lap, lap, lap* of her tongue. You hold your breath.

Cassandra turns and faces the crowd of anxious cats. "As you can see, it's perfectly safe to drink."

"Thank goodness," Victoria says, voicing everyone's thoughts. The rest of the cats cheer.

Augustus turns to you. "Once again you've saved us, my friend."

You nod gravely. "I didn't do much," you insist. "The real credit goes to Cassandra. She was the one who uncovered the source of the problem."

"You're right," Augustus agrees. "We've been so afraid of Cassandra's prophecies that we've been refusing to listen. And we've made her an outcast for trying to help us." He turns to Cassandra. "Can you forgive us?" he asks.

"Of course," she says. "This makes me very happy."

It's a very touching scene. You turn to see how your new friend, Leo, is reacting. He's always been right by your side. But now he's nowhere in sight!

Victoria notices, at the same time as you do, that Leo is gone.

"Leo, Leo," she calls.

He doesn't answer.

Moments later, you and the whole cat population are scouring the caverns looking for the wayward kitten. But he's nowhere to be found. You get a funny feeling in your stomach. Suppose that crazy kid has wandered off outside the cave.

"Would you like me to see if I can summon up a vision?" Cassandra asks.

"Oh, would you please? I'd be so grate-ful," Victoria tells her.

Cassandra crouches down, wraps her tail around her body, and closes her eyes. When she starts to speak, her voice seems to be coming from far away. "I see a field. It's the meadow in front of Castle Mountain." She pauses and gives a little meow. "Leo is there."

"Oh, he's safe," Victoria sighs.

But Cassandra seems not to hear her. "I sense danger," she continues. "We must get to Leo fast."

In a flash, the cats head toward the field. You're right behind them. The only thought on your mind is to rescue your friend before it's too late.

In the field, you all spread out to look for the missing kitten. A flicker of move-ment in the direction of Queen Cerise's castle catches your attention. Two of the queen's vicious dogs are streaking across the field. You hear them bark. Then you hear a small, scared-sounding meow. Oh no! They've cornered Leo.

You dash toward him at top speed. But you're too late. One of the dogs has a bundle of orange fur in his mouth. He and his companion turn and head back to the queen's castle.

You stumble to the place where you last saw Leo. All that remains is the little collar Leo wore around his neck.

Chapter 5

The cats gather around the scene of the kit-napping. Leo's mother is trying to be brave. But you can tell that her eyes are brimming with tears. The two warriors, Justinian and Brutus, are all for storming the castle walls. But the wise Augustus disagrees.

"We need cunning, not force," Augustus says.

"Yes, we need to get someone into the queen's castle," Isis suggests. "Someone whom she won't suspect is there to rescue Leo. Maybe one of us could dress up like a dog."

Augustus shakes his head. "That would never work. Even if the queen could be fooled, the dogs would smell an impostor."

"What you really need is someone who's not a cat," you suggest.

All eyes turn in your direction.

"Would you be willing to do something that dangerous?" Victoria asks in a quiet voice.

"Yes," you say bravely. Although you manage to keep your features calm, your heart is pounding double time. You've seen enough of Queen Cerise to know that she's ruthless and cruel. But you can't stand to think of poor little Leo in the clutches of the Red Queen. You know you must try to save him.

Augustus leads the way back to Castle Mountain. "We've been spying on Queen Cerise for a long time, and we know she loves to get important visitors from foreign lands," he says. "We'll dress you up to look like a noble traveler from far away.

That way you should have no trouble getting into her good graces.

"It would also be good if you could claim to have some special powers. That would make her really interested," he adds. "In fact, the more magical, the better. Our wicked queen has always coveted the power of magic. Unluckily for her, but luckily for us, she's all thumbs when it comes to spells. They never work out quite the way she plans."

At that moment, the Magic Micro springs to life.

No problem with the magical powers bit. We can handle that. With my help, she'll think you're the greatest magician since Houdini.

Augustus and the other cats lead you to a room deep inside the mountain that is full of fabulously rich-looking clothing. "The Masters left all this," Augustus explains. "Up till now, we've had no use for any of it. But something in here should be perfect for your disguise."

You inspect a variety of velvet, satin, and brocade outfits, but finally settle on an emerald-green silk tunic with a wide, diamond-studded belt. Black tights and pointed slippers complete the outfit. You strut back and forth in front of the mirror, impressed with your image.

"You look very important," says Cassandra. Her words remind you that there's more to this than just donning a bunch of neat clothes. "Will my mission be successful?" you ask her.

"I think it would be better not to make you either overconfident or despairing," she says, dodging your question. "Really, you are the master of your own fate."

You know she's right. But still, you wanted to hear her say that this is all going to be all right in the end.

The cats bid you a solemn good-bye. Victoria rubs her nose gently against yours for good luck. Then, with a mixture of fear and excitement, you set off across the meadow toward the castle. It still looks like something out of a fairy tale. The shiny rooftops reflect the sun. And the colorful banners wave proudly in the wind. You remember wanting to go to the castle when you first arrived here. But, of course, that was before you knew who lived there.

There's no point in looking back. You march toward the drawbridge at the entrance of the castle. Six large Dobermans are standing at the end of the drawbridge nearest you. Several bare their teeth and snarl. You'd like to turn around and go back. But you must rescue Leo. And if *you're* scared, you remind yourself, *he* must be terrified in there all alone with the queen and her dogs.

As you approach, one dog steps forward and starts sniffing your clothes. Do they smell like cats? Are your clothes going to give you away?

"Take me to Queen Cerise," you demand boldly. "She will be very angry with you if you insult me. I am an important visitor from far away."

The dogs don't want to anger their mistress. The head dog motions for you to follow him. Your footsteps sound loud to you as you cross the drawbridge.

Inside the castle, you look around with interest. The castle is decorated in red and black. The stone floor is cold and gray. The furniture is heavy and dark and uncomfortable looking. The only light is provided by a few dim candles.

The dog leads you down a winding stone hallway toward the back of the castle. He pauses and pulls a bell cord with his teeth.

"Enter," a voice commands. The voice is all too familiar.

The dog steps aside and nudges you forward. With hands that tremble slightly, you pull open the heavy oak door and step into the queen's throne room.

The first thing that catches your eye is a large silver cage in the corner of the room. It's hanging suspended near the ceiling. Leo is inside, pacing back and forth. When he sees you, he stops and his mouth falls open in surprise. Quickly you give your head a slight shake. You hope he's smart enough not to blow your cover.

You tear your eyes away from your imprisoned friend and look in the direction of the queen. She is dressed in a red silk gown and is sitting on a throne at the end of the hall. Her long red nails match her outfit. You can see that she's working on a piece of needlepoint. For a few moments she doesn't bother to raise her eyes from her work. You glance around at the samples of her work hanging on the wall.

One says: THE ONLY GOOD CAT IS A CATSKIN RUG.

The queen finally acknowledges you. She tips her head to one side and looks you over from head to toe. Suddenly you're very glad to be dressed as finely as she is.

"Yes. What can you do for me?" she asks.

"I'm a great and powerful traveler from a distant land," you say, hoping your voice carries the right conviction. After all, you're not really lying. You *are* from pretty far away. And you have the power of the Magic Micro tucked in the pocket of your tunic.

She looks interested. You see her sit up straighter and adjust the silver crown on her head. "Won't you join me for tea?" she asks, a greedy smile curling her lips.

"Delighted," you answer.

The two of you sit down at an elaborately carved table. When she rings a bell, two dogs come in almost at once, pushing a tea cart filled with all sorts of goodies.

"What kind of Danish pastry would you like?" she asks in a sweet, high-pitched voice.

"Cheese Danish is my favorite."

The queen looks startled and peers at you suspiciously.

"No cheese!" she exclaims, strangely upset.

"That's all right," you say. "Cherry will do fine."

Queen Cerise relaxes again. As she serves you tea and sweets, she begins to chat about her rose garden and favorite charities, like the Doberman Pension Fund.

"It's so nice to have someone to talk to,"

she says. And if you didn't know better, you'd be taken in by her sugary perform- ance. But you only have to glance up in the corner of the room and see Leo in his cage to know that the queen isn't what she's pretending to be.

"How are things going in the king- dom?" you ask casually.

She shakes her head and sighs. "You know, this is such a tough job. Sometimes you get no respect. Take the cats who live not a mile from this very castle. They're driving me up the wall. They don't obey my laws. They're destroying my trees. And they don't pay a penny in rent."

Out of the corner of your eye, you can see Leo hissing and jumping up and down. But you pretend to sympathize with the queen's plight.

You look down modestly. "I do know a bit of magic. Maybe I can help you," you suggest.

"Magic?" she squeaks. You can see she's trying to hide her eagerness. But she can't keep her beady eyes from lighting up. "Oh, I'd do anything to get rid of this cat problem once and for all," she says sweetly. "Help me and anything you want is yours."

"I'd be glad to help you get just what you deserve," you say. Then you look casually over at Leo's cage. "Is this one of the offenders?" you ask.

"Yes, I captured him only this morning," the queen explains. "I'm keeping him around to get information from him before tossing him to my dogs."

"Well, let me use him to show you a nifty magic trick," you offer.

The queen can hardly control her excitement. "I'd love to see a demonstration of your powers," she says.

You pull out the Magic Micro. "I channel my power through this," you say.

The queen doesn't seem to find that unusual, and you breath a sigh of relief.

Just to make everything look authentic, you wave your arms like a magician, then you do your *real* magic.

Type the following program into your computer. Then turn to pages 74-76 and type in the lines listed for your computer. When you have finished typing, run the program. It will lower Leo's cage to the ground so that he can escape.

PROGRAM 4

```
10   GOSUB 900: GOSUB 960
20   A=SH-8:B=1
30   TL$="   !    ":T$="+--!--+"
40   SD$="!        !":B$="+-Leo-+"
50   BL$="           "
60   HT= INT(SW/4)
70   VT=2:GOSUB 910:PRINT TL$
80   VT=3
90   GOSUB 910: PRINT TL$:VT=VT+1
100   GOSUB 910: PRINT T$:VT=VT+1
110   FOR I=1 TO 3
120   GOSUB 910: PRINT SD$
130   VT=VT+1
140   NEXT I
150   GOSUB 910: PRINT B$:VT=VT+1
160   FOR I=3 TO A
170   GOSUB 200
180   NEXT I
190   END
200   VT=I: GOSUB 910
210   PRINT TL$:VT=VT+1
220   GOSUB 910: PRINT T$
230   VT=VT+1: GOSUB 910: PRINT SD$
240   VT=I+5: GOSUB 910: PRINT SD$
250   VT=VT+1: GOSUB 910: PRINT B$
260   RETURN
```

The queen stares in disbelief as you open the door and Leo streaks out of the cage and through the open window. You watch him jump to the first-floor roof and down to the ground. In a moment, he's running across the meadow, back to Castle Mountain.

"You'll pay for this!" screams the queen.

Chapter 6

"Didn't I make that cat disappear?" you ask innocently. You wish the Magic Micro had explained how you were going to bluff your way out of the castle after putting on your little show.

"Give me that magic box you're holding," Queen Cerise demands, lunging forward.

You cross your arms protectively over the Magic Micro and take a step backward. "It's much too dangerous for anyone but me," you protest.

"You're lying," the queen shrieks. She continues to advance and you retreat until your back is pressed against the cold stone wall.

"What are you going to do to me?" you ask.

The queen only laughs and pulls a lever concealed behind a drapery. Suddenly the floor beneath your feet gives way and you're falling, falling, falling. You hit the floor with so much force that the breath is knocked out of you. Only the pile of straw on the cold stones keeps you from serious injury.

When you come to your senses, you look around. You're in a dark, musty room. It must be the dungeon of the castle. A single shaft of light is coming from above. You look up and see the hole you fell through. Queen Cerise is glaring down at you.

"So you thought you could fool me. Well, you have to get up pretty early in the morning for that!" she sneers. "Those miserable cats must have sent you. I should let you rot down there."

"Won't that ruin your reputation as a hostess?" you ask.

The queen pauses to think about your

question. "You may have a point," she answers. "Never let it be said that I'm not a sporting person. I'm going to give you a chance to get out of my dungeon."

Your ears perk up.

"Don't get too excited," she cackles. "No one's ever escaped yet. But I've had so much fun watching them try."

You shudder. You suspect that her idea of a good time isn't the same as yours.

"Let me tell you the rules of the game," she continues. "You'll notice that there are nine doors arranged around the dungeon."

You look around. In the dim light, you can make out the doors. In fact, they have numbers from 1 to 9 painted on them.

"I have gold and jewels hidden behind some of the doors," she explains. "If you collect enough of them, I'll let you buy your way out. But beware. Two of the doors lead to my alligator pit. Of course, if you pick either one, you'll be their supper."

Suddenly the Magic Micro beeps.

I think I can help with this, it says. You certainly hope so!

Carefully type the following program into your computer. (Lines 110, 160, 170, 180, and 190 must each be typed as one line.) When you have typed these lines, turn to pages 77-78 and type in the lines listed for your computer. Run the program. The Magic Scroll on page 79 will tell you how to play Queen Cerise's deadly game.

PROGRAM 5

```
10 GOSUB 960
20 DIM D(9)
30 FOR I=1 TO 9
40 D(I)=100
50 NEXT I
60 FOR I=1 TO 2
70 RX=9:GOSUB 930
80 D(RD)=0
90 NEXT I
100 PRINT "PICK ANY DOOR 1 - 9"
110 PRINT "IF IT'S ONE YOU'VE
    ALREADY TRIED YOU'LL LOSE
    POINTS"
120 INPUT P
130 IF D(P)=0 THEN 180
140 S=S+D(P):D(P)=-100
150 IF S =>500 THEN 170
160 PRINT "YOUR SCORE IS:",S:
    GOTO 100
170 PRINT "YOU'VE GOT ENOUGH GOLD
    TO GET OUT": END
180 PRINT "BEHIND THIS DOOR IS A
    HUNGRY ALLIGATOR"
190 PRINT "HE'S DELIGHTED THAT YOU
    STOPPED IN FOR SUPPER."
200 END
```

Thank goodness you did it! But before you can make your escape, a tenth door hidden in the stone wall opens, and Queen Cerise steps into the dungeon.

Gasping, you jump back. "I thought you were going to let me go," you protest.

"Don't expect me to play fair with you. After all, you didn't play fair with me," she rasps, her nose twitching.

Even though that seems logical, you don't like the way it sounds.

"If you give me that magic box of yours, I might let you go," she offers, advancing toward you menacingly.

You clutch the Magic Micro to your chest. Besides being your friend, it's your only ticket home.

Just then, you see something at the edge of the trap door above. It's Leo, Cassandra, and a half dozen other cats. They're all holding chunks of cheese between their teeth and they stand above the queen. As you watch, they drop the pieces of cheese on her.

"How is this going to help?" you ask yourself.

As the first chunk of cheese hits the queen, she shrieks, "Oh no!"

Next, as you watch open-mouthed, red fog begins to swirl about Queen Cerise. Soon it's covering her like a cloud. You can't see what's happening in there. And you're not sure you'd want to. All you know is that her shrieks have somehow turned to squeaks.

When the fog disappears, a frightened mouse is cowering where the queen was standing. Around it on the floor are Queen Cerise's false fingernails and high-heeled shoes.

As you watch, the mouse scurries for a hole in the dungeon wall.

"Hooray, we've broken the spell," Augustus shouts from above.

"Cassandra was right!" Caesar adds.

You look at her questioningly. "What spell?"

"The truth came to me in a vision this

morning right after you left," Cassandra explains. "Cerise was a mouse all along. But somehow she persuaded a wizard to turn her into a queen. He did it. But he made her give up the thing she loved the most — cheese! Any contact with cheese would break the spell and turn her back into a mouse."

"Lucky for me you had that vision," you say.

The Magic Micro beeps in agreement. *Lucky for all of us*, the screen flashes.

You nod and start to climb the stairs back to the throne room. But when you step through the red velvet curtain, you almost fall over one of the queen's guard dogs.

"Is it true the queen is gone?" he asks.

"Well . . . um . . ." you stammer.

"It's okay," Cassandra assures you. "My vision also told me the dogs were loyal to the queen only because they were afraid of her. They're as happy to see the last of her as we are."

"We like the way you stood up to the

queen," the head dog says to you. "We need a leader now. Why don't you take over the castle?"

"I appreciate the honor," you tell him, "but I must be getting back home."

All the cats look disappointed. "We'll miss you," Leo says.

You look at the little orange kitten that started this whole adventure. "I'll miss you, too," you whisper. You look around at the group of cats. "I'll always remember all of you," you say.

It's time to go, the Magic Micro says.

There's that old familiar flash, and suddenly you're back home in your bed again. Your gray and white cat comes over and butts his head against your arm as if he's thanking you just the way Leo did. You give him an affectionate scratch under the chin. Every time you look at him, you'll remember the Cats of Castle Mountain.

Magic Scroll

The Magic Scroll is here to help you. Flip through the next few pages. Find the heading for the kind of computer you are using. The Magic Scroll will tell you what lines to add and what lines to take out to make each program run on your computer. The Magic Scroll will also tell you a little bit about each computer.

PROGRAM 1

Changes:

If you have an IBM PC or PCjr, add these lines to Program 1. (Line 960 must be typed as one line.)

```
900  CLS:RETURN
910  LOCATE VT,HT:RETURN
930  RD=INT(RND*RX)+1:RETURN
960  SH=24:SW=78:AC=39:AS=174:
     MU=1900:RETURN
980  SOUND RD+50,6:RETURN
```

If you have a Commodore 64, add these
lines to Program 1. (Lines 910 and 960
must each be typed as one line.) Also
remove line 60.

```
900 PRINT CHR$(147);:RETURN
910 POKE XT,HT-1:POKE YT:
    POKE FG,0:SYS PL:RETURN
930 RD=INT(RX*RND(1)+1):RETURN
960 SW=40:SH=24:AC=30:AS=96:
    XT=782:YT=781:FG=783:PL=65520:
    RETURN
980 POKE 54296,15
982 POKE 54273,34:POKE 54272,75:
984 POKE 54273,0:POKE 54272,0:
985 FOR K1=1 TO 20:NEXT K1
986 RETURN
```

If you have a VIC-20, add these lines to
Program 1. (Lines 910 and 960 must each
be typed as one line.)

```
900 PRINT CHR$(147);:RETURN
910 POKE XT,HT-1:POKE YT:
    POKE FG,0:SYS PL:RETURN
930 RD=INT(RX*RND(1)+1):RETURN
960 SW=22:SH=22:AC=30:AS=96:
    XT=782:YT=781:FG=783:PL=65520:
    MU=120:RETURN
980 POKE 36878,15
982 POKE 36874,RD+128:RETURN
```

If you have a Radio Shack TRS-80, add these lines to Program 1. (Lines 910 and 960 must each be typed as one line.) Also remove lines 60 and 70.

```
900 CLS:RETURN
910 HZ=INT(HT-1+(VT-1)*SW+0.5):
    PRINT @HZ,"";:RETURN
930 RD=INT(RND(RX)):RETURN
960 SW=64:SH=16:AC=30:AS=33:
    MU=255:RETURN
980 RETURN
```

If you have a Radio Shack Color Computer, add these lines to Program 1. (Lines 910 and 960 must each be typed as one line.) Requires extended BASIC.

```
900 CLS:RETURN
910 HZ=INT(HT-1+(VT-1)*SW+0.5):
    PRINT @HZ,"";:RETURN
930 RD=INT(RND(RX)):RETURN
960 SW=32:SH=16:AC=12:AS=128:
    MU=255:RETURN
980 SOUND RD,5:RETURN
```

If you have an Atari, add these lines to
Program 1. (Line 960 must be typed as
one line.)

```
900 PRINT CHR$(125):RETURN
910 POSITION VT-1,HT+1:RETURN
930 RD=INT(RND(0)*RX+1):RETURN
960 SW=38:SH=24:AC=25:
    AS=128:MU=255:RETURN
980 SOUND 0,RD,10,8
985 SOUND 0,0,0,0:RETURN
```

If you have an Apple II + or Apple IIe,
add these lines to Program 1. Also remove line 60.

```
900 HOME:RETURN
910 VTAB(VT):HTAB(HT):RETURN
930 RD=INT(RND(1)*RX+1):RETURN
960 SW=38:SH=24:AC=30:AS=33:RETURN
980 PRINT CHR$(7):RETURN
```

About the program:

When you type in your destination and
press ENTER, the flashing lights and
music transport you right to Castle
Mountain. To do this, the program gen-
erates 150 random sounds and 150 random characters on the screen.

PROGRAM 2

Changes:

If you have an IBM PC or PCjr, add these lines to Program 2. (Line 970 must be typed as one line.)

```
900  CLS:RETURN
910  LOCATE VT,HT:RETURN
930  RD=INT(RX*RND+1):RETURN
960  SW=40:SH=24:RETURN
970  RANDOMIZE(VAL(RIGHT$(
     TIME$,2))):RETURN
```

If you have an Apple II+ or Apple IIe, add these lines to Program 2.

```
900  HOME:RETURN
910  VTAB(VT):HTAB(HT):RETURN
920  FOR WS=1 TO WT:RETURN
930  RD=INT(RND(1)*RX+1):RETURN
960  SW=38:SH=24:AC=30:AS=33:RETURN
```

If you have an Atari, add these lines to Program 2.

```
900  PRINT CHR$(125):RETURN
910  POSITION VT-1,HT+1:RETURN
930  RD=INT(RND(0)*RX+1):RETURN
960  SW=38:SH=24:RETURN
```

If you have a Radio Shack TRS- 80, add these lines to Program 2. (Line 910 must be typed as one line.)

```
900 CLS:RETURN
910 HZ=INT(HT-1+(VT-1)*SW+0.5):
    PRINT @HZ,"";:RETURN
930 RD=INT(RND(RX)):RETURN
960 SW=64:SH=16:RETURN
```

If you have a Radio Shack Color Computer, add these lines to Program 2. (Line 910 must be typed as one line.)

```
900 CLS:RETURN
910 HZ=INT(HT-1+(VT-1)*SW+0.5):
    PRINT @HZ,"";:RETURN
930 RD=INT(RND(RX)):RETURN
960 SW=32:SH=16:RETURN
```

If you have a Commodore 64, add these lines to Program 2. (Line 910 must be typed as one line.)

```
900 PRINT CHR$(147);:RETURN
910 POKE 782,HT-1:POKE 781:VT-1:
    POKE 783,0:SYS 65520:RETURN
930 RD=INT(RX*RND(1)+1):RETURN
960 SW=40:SH=24:RETURN
970 RD=RND(-TI):RETURN
```

If you have a VIC-20, add these lines to Program 2. (Line 910 must be typed as one line.)

```
900 PRINT CHR$(147);:RETURN
910 POKE 782,HT-1:POKE 781:VT-1:
    POKE 783,0:SYS 65520:RETURN
930 RD=INT(RX*RND(1)+1):RETURN
960 SW=20:SH=22:RETURN
970 RD=RND(-TI):RETURN
```

About the program:

The way to make the stars come out is by knowing your math. The Magic Micro will give you a series of sums to add up. Each time you get an answer right, you will get as many stars as the answer. For example, if you answer 11 when the Magic Micro asks you to add 6 and 5, you will be right and 11 stars will come out. If you say 12, you will be wrong and you will lose. The Magic Micro will let you know when you've got enough stars to strengthen the force field.

PROGRAM 3

Changes:

If you have an IBM PC or PCjr, add these lines to Program 3. (Lines 960 and 970 must each be typed as one line.)

```
900 CLS:RETURN
910 LOCATE VT,HT:RETURN
930 RD=INT(RND*RX)+1:RETURN
960 SH=24:SW=40:WT=100:
    GOSUB 970:RETURN
970 RANDOMIZE(VAL(RIGHT$(
    TIME$,2))):RETURN
```

If you have an Apple II+ or Apple IIe, add these lines to Program 3.

```
900 HOME:RETURN
910 VTAB(VT):HTAB(HT):RETURN
930 RD=INT(RND(1)*RX+1):RETURN
960 SW=38:SH=24:RETURN
```

If you have an Atari, add these lines to Program 3.

```
900 PRINT CHR$(125):RETURN
910 POSITION VT-1,HT+1:RETURN
930 RD=INT(RND(0)*RX+1):RETURN
960 SW=38:SH=24:RETURN
```

If you have a Commodore 64, add these lines to Program 3. (Line 910 must be typed as one line.)

```
900 PRINT CHR$(147);:RETURN
910 POKE 782,HT-1:POKE 781:VT-1:
    POKE 783,0:SYS 65520:RETURN
930 RD=INT(RX*RND(1)+1):RETURN
960 SW=40:SH=24:GOSUB 970:RETURN
970 RD=RND(-TI):RETURN
```

If you have a Radio Shack TRS-80, add these lines to Program 3. (Line 910 must be typed as one line.)

```
900 CLS:RETURN
910 HZ=INT(HT-1+(VT-1)*SW+0.5):
    PRINT @HZ,"";:RETURN
930 RD=INT(RND(RX)):RETURN
960 SW=64:SH=16:RETURN
```

If you have a Radio Shack Color Computer, add these lines to Program 3. (Line 910 must be typed as one line.)

```
900 CLS:RETURN
910 HZ=INT(HT-1+(VT-1)*SW+0.5):
    PRINT @HZ,"";:RETURN
930 RD=INT(RND(RX)):RETURN
960 SW=32:SH=16:RETURN
```

If you have a VIC-20, add these lines to Program 3. (Line 910 must be typed as one line.)

```
900 PRINT CHR$(147);:RETURN
910 POKE 782,HT-1:POKE 781:VT-1:
    POKE 783,0:SYS 65520:RETURN
930 RD=INT(RX*RND(1)+1):RETURN
960 SW=20:SH=22:GOSUB 970:RETURN
960 RD=RND(-TI):RETURN
```

About the program:

Wicked Queen Cerise has added chemicals to the cats' drinking water. Unless you can adjust the filtering system to neutralize the chemical, the cats will grow weak and they will have to surrender when Cerise attacks. To adjust the filter, type in a number between 1 and 100 to set the filter's dial. Your Magic Micro will tell you if you are too high or too low. Keep readjusting the dial until you have exactly the right setting to make the water drinkable. The Magic Micro will tell you when it is right. Choose your settings carefully. The filtering system is very old, and if you adjust it more than seven times, it will break.

PROGRAM 4

Changes:

If you have an IBM PC or PCjr, add
these lines to Program 4.

```
900  CLS:RETURN
910  LOCATE VT,HT:RETURN
960  SH=24:SW=78:RETURN
```

If you have a Commodore 64, add these
lines to Program 4. (Line 910 must be
typed as one line.)

```
900 PRINT CHR$(147);:RETURN
910 POKE 782,HT-1:POKE 781:VT-1:
    POKE 783,0:SYS 65520:RETURN
960 SW=40:SH=24:RETURN
```

If you have an Apple II + or Apple IIe,
add these lines to Program 4.

```
900 HOME:RETURN
910 VTAB(VT):HTAB(HT):RETURN
960 SW=38:SH=24:RETURN
```

If you have a Radio Shack TRS-80, add these lines to Program 4. (Line 910 must be typed as one line.)

```
900 CLS:RETURN
910 HZ=INT(HT-1+(VT-1)*SW+0.5):
    PRINT @HZ,"";:RETURN
960 SW=64:SH=16:RETURN
```

If you have a Radio Shack Color Computer, add these lines to Program 4. (Line 910 must be typed as one line.)

```
900 CLS:RETURN
910 HZ=INT(HT-1+(VT-1)*SW+0.5):
    PRINT @HZ,"";:RETURN
960 SW=32:SH=16:RETURN
```

If you have an Atari, add these lines to Program 4.

```
900 PRINT CHR$(125):RETURN
910 POSITION VT-1,HT+1:RETURN
960 SW=38:SH=24:RETURN
```

If you have a VIC-20, add these lines to Program 4. (Line 910 must be typed as one line.)

```
900 PRINT CHR$(147);:RETURN
910 POKE 782,HT-1:POKE 781:VT-1:
    POKE 783,0:SYS 65520:RETURN
960 SW=20:SH=24:RETURN
```

About the program:

Use this program to lower Leo's cage to the ground so he can escape. Just type in the lines, and the Magic Micro will do the rest.

PROGRAM 5

Changes:

If you have an IBM PC or PCjr, add these lines to Program 5. (Line 970 must be typed as one line.)

```
930 RD=INT(RND*RX)+1:RETURN
960 SH=24:SW=40:GOSUB 970:RETURN
970 RANDOMIZE(VAL(RIGHT$(
    TIME$,2))):RETURN
```

If you have a VIC-20, add these lines to Program 5.

```
930 RD=INT(RX*RND(1)+1):RETURN
960 SW=40:SH=24:GOSUB 970:RETURN
970 RD=RND(-TI):RETURN
```

If you have a Commodore 64, add these lines to Program 5.

```
930 RD=INT(RX*RND(1)+1):RETURN
960 SW=20:SH=22:GOSUB 970:RETURN
970 RD=RND(-TI):RETURN
```

If you have an Apple II+ or Apple IIe, add these lines to Program 5.

```
930 RD=INT(RND(1)*RX+1):RETURN
960 SW=38:SH=24:RETURN
```

If you have a Radio Shack TRS-80, add these lines to Program 5.

```
930 RD=INT(RND(RX)):RETURN
960 SW=64:SH=16:RETURN
```

If you have a Radio Shack Color Computer, add these lines to Program 5.

```
930 RD=INT(RND(RX)):RETURN
960 SW=32:SH=16:RETURN
```

If you have an Atari, add these lines to Program 5.

```
930 RD=INT(RND(0)*RX+1):RETURN
960 SW=38:SH=24:RETURN
```

About the program:

Queen Cerise is playing games with you and it could cost you your life. You are down in the dungeon. There are nine doors. Behind seven of the doors are bags containing 100 gold coins. Behind an eighth and a ninth door are hungry alligators. You must collect 500 gold coins in order to buy your freedom. So pick any door from 1 to 9 and find out what's waiting for you there.